T0130129

Also by Patti Angeletti (as Patti Murphy)

Rising Above Organized Religion: The Journey to the Higher View

PREFLIGHT
A Soul Prepares to Return to Earth

Patti Angeletti

iUniverse, Inc.
New York   Bloomington

Preflight
A Soul Prepares to Return to Earth

Copyright © 2009 Patti Angeletti

This is a work of fiction. All of the characters, names, incidents,
organizations, and dialogue in this novel are either the products
of the author's imagination or are used fictitiously.

iUniverse books may be ordered through booksellers or by contacting:

iUniverse
1663 Liberty Drive
Bloomington, IN 47403
www.iuniverse.com
1-800-Authors (1-800-288-4677)

ISBN: 978-1-4401-7042-3 (pbk)
ISBN: 978-1-4401-7044-7 (cloth)
ISBN: 978-1-4401-7043-0 (ebk)

Printed in the United States of America

iUniverse rev. date: 9/14/2009

In memory of my parents and others in spirit

Each of us is here to discover our true Self ... that essentially we are spiritual beings who have taken manifestation in physical form ... that we're not human beings that have occasional spiritual experiences ... that we're spiritual beings that have occasional human experiences.

—Deepak Chopra

To my daughter Jami, whose musical expertise, love, and support have helped in ways I would not have believed possible.

To my personal angels and guides, whose constant influence made the work a joy.

To David Hays and Po, whose spirits live on.

To my musically talented friends Michael, Sean, Cindy, Russ, Jamie, Sue, Mark, Hugh, and many others who made the music possible.

To Rebecca, who has given the gift of her lullaby to the world.

CONTENTS

INTRODUCTION

To benefit, in any regard, from reading this book, simply open your heart and mind to the possibilities. From a practical point of view, the story is pure fantasy. But why not think somewhere beyond practical?

I do not believe in coincidence or accidents. I believe each encounter we have with a person or situation has been planned and orchestrated. I believe in learning more about myself and my choices in life, looking for a deeper meaning in the interactions I have with others, in the places I find myself, and even in the day-to-day and moment-to-moment events I experience.

When you believe that what you experience has been created by you, you will find yourself beginning to take more responsibility for your actions and words, and ultimately designing a more satisfying existence.

As you read this book, imagine it to be a musical. The stage is set, there is dialogue and interaction between characters before a song is introduced, and someone sings from her heart and soul. I believe we all have a soundtrack to our lives. At the end of specific chapters, this book includes Sarah's Preflight soundtrack.

Because this book could not be without music, without the Lullaby, a music CD is available for purchase that may add to your enjoyment of *Preflight*. Contact me at sequeltosarah@yahoo.com for more information. Music brings the world together.

PREFACE:
THE LULLABY

Within all of us, there is an elusive melody,
which, when heard and followed, will lead us
to the fulfillment of our fondest dreams.

—Announcer at final Siegfried and Roy performance

Many on Earth remember the Lullaby the moment they hear
it—a vaguely familiar melody that touches the soul. They could
be considered lucky, but they are not the only ones who can
experience it. Anyone can, because the Lullaby is everywhere.
How do I know? I know because I am an angel.

I hear the Lullaby all the time. It never ends. Actually, it
never began either. It has always existed. It is as timeless and far-
reaching as the most distant star and as deep as the basic elements
of existence. Some beings are able to hear it everywhere while
traveling through space and time; there is no space in which it
is not.

On Earth, I experience its tones and chords in rocks,
mountains, and trees. Perhaps you have, too. Have you ever sat

on a beach, closed your eyes, and really listened to the waves as they gently curled, tumbled, and flowed on the sand? Have you really heard the gentle tinkling of chimes in a gentle breeze? How about the coos and laughter of a baby, or the purrs of a cat? The Lullaby can be found in each of these. Sometimes it takes just a little effort and fine-tuning to hear it amid the noise.

It is natural for me to hear the Lullaby. It is like a symphony of crystal violin strings, a flowing and melding of tones and harmonies. Occasionally, there is a sound like the wind through the leaves, like an echo of laughter, or like a murmur of whispers, as gentle and soft as flower petals on your cheek or fine silk upon your shoulders.

I see the Lullaby as well. It is an amazing display of shimmering substance, ever moving and creating itself into new shapes and colors, hues I cannot even begin to describe. It has brilliant greens and blues, intense reds and yellows, and the softest of pinks, all with a sort of glow about them.

The color scheme is endless, and many of the colors don't exist on Earth. Your human eyes would not be able to see them; that is even more true since everything about experiencing the Lullaby is influenced by love—something that isn't always evident on Earth. The more love you have, however, the more love you give, and the more love you see in the things around you—and then, the more you can hear and feel and see of the Lullaby. It's as simple as that.

Acting out of love by sharing, smiling, and encouraging others helps you fine-tune the person you are, and you become more sensitive to the tones and melody. Being selfish or hurting others in any way, even simply being afraid, brings more static and noise, making the Lullaby more difficult to hear.

With love, however, anyone can *feel* the Lullaby, not just hear it. Experiencing the Lullaby within the heart and soul, in the very core of your being, brings a true sense of peace like no other, a sense of belonging, connectedness, and eternity, and one of creation, completeness, and oneness. Sensing the Lullaby is feeling pure love and the kind of emotion that brings tears to your eyes and causes your chest to feel like it could burst with joy. Or so I am told. Because I am an angel, my understanding is different from a soul within a human form.

There is another way, however, besides showing love. Those who have learned to sit in quiet meditation and tune out the noise around them can experience the Lullaby in a beautiful and simple way.

When souls decide to come to Earth, their journeys can cause them to forget the Lullaby so completely that they claim it doesn't exist. Many hear it occasionally, believing they are hallucinating or dreaming. Others may have heard it once but have since disconnected themselves from love and thus the Lullaby, ending up feeling lost and alone; even then, however, a few tones of the Lullaby can lift them up, put peace in their hearts, and give them hope.

The Lullaby has amazing powers. It helps everything grow: plants, animals, insects, fish ... well, everything! It supplies strength to the trunks of trees and gentleness to the wings of butterflies. It imparts the subtle scents of flowers.

Experiencing the Lullaby can be a soul's moment of truth—a

profound, heartfelt moment, containing wonder and remembrance. It can be the best "ah-ha" moment ever! The moment you realize that it is the Lullaby that brings all things together and is a part of all things. A moment that reminds you of the One Love, pure and strong, that exists for everyone and everything, the One Love that binds all together.

For this moment, you must listen carefully and watch, for the Lullaby glows within the eyes of those who know its secret. See it and listen with your heart.

Chapter 1
What Angels Are About

Areanna

Yes, I am an angel. I am not the kind with wings, but if thinking of wings helps you imagine me, then go right ahead. Place on my shoulders a nice set of white wings made of iridescent feathers tipped in gold, if you please. Just make sure they fan out in a manner that is grand and glorious. It really doesn't matter what you think I look like, what color hair I may have, or what style of dress I might wear. (Though, just so you know, not all of us are predominantly female, so not all of us wear dresses. Think of Archangel Michael. A dress wouldn't suit him, I think.)

Anyway, none of these Earthly physical attributes make any difference to me. They're just not important. I'm just happy to be what I am—a glowing, loving magnificent essence. As energy, I am able to travel at the speed of thought (so I don't need wings to get around). And though I can fit inside the smallest space you can imagine, I can also expand to immense proportions. I have mastered the art of disguise in your world. I can look like anyone, perform any task, and speak any language. This is a handy talent when needing to blend in.

I have seen some of the human art created throughout the centuries of what you believe or hope angels look like. The depictions are really quite interesting. Many artists may have rendered such images because they remember glimpses of the spirit world, or have the gift to see us, or because we have appeared to them in dreams. Just as in art, we do not all appear the same. We can take on many forms, sizes, and colors. I am known as Areanna, at least in the way you speak on Earth. If I said (or even spelled) my name for you in Original Language or Angel Speak, your human way of hearing sounds could not make any sense of it. Angel Speak is a beautiful language and very exotic. It is a combination of musical tones mixed with love. It can sound flowing and majestic or quiet like a whisper, similar to the beating of butterfly wings. I would guess that you have heard an angel speak to you at some time in your life. I hope you recognized it as something special.

I have one of the best occupations in the Universe. It isn't really a job in the way you might think of. My employment is Who I Am; it's just what I do. I love and serve. It is what I was meant to do from before the beginning and what I will continue to do forever. It is wonderful. I serve along with a host of angels and other masters here on the side of creation that many on Earth have forgotten about.

As a Guardian angel, I do what I am asked to do, plain and simple. Ask or command, and I am there. At times, requests for assistance may be delayed or altered a bit, depending on what is best for the soul at the time. People have been warned to be careful about what they ask for, because the results aren't always quite what they have in mind or what they are ready for. For example, some who have won lottery money have lost it all again quite quickly. So, know that angels are there to help you, and that we exhibit amazing physical strength, but some of the grander commands may not be for your highest good. Often, we must allow what is to happen in order for the soul to learn its lessons. Also, some things you are capable of doing yourself. We stay very busy, as you might imagine. There are many ways we accomplish what we are asked to do at any given moment. We can inspire or instruct other humans to help. We can summon the help of any element or creature, cause rain to fall or the sun to shine. We may appear as human beings on Earth for a brief time or longer. Those who have can relate very well to the restraints placed on a physical body and the suffering it can endure. They usually assist those in their families and many times are recognized in photographs.

In the hierarchy of the angelic realm, there are others with more experience and knowledge than I, with different responsibilities. Their roles vary according to level, but they can always assist Guardian angels, if necessary. Other levels of angels may be called Seraphim, Cherubim, Thrones, Dominions, Virtues, Powers, Principalities, and Archangels. There may be other names, but these seem the most common terms used on Earth.

What angels know generally covers two categories: love and service. What we do not know covers only one category: fear. Fear is simply the absence of love. Without love, humans will feel (and show) hate, envy, anger, greed, shame, apathy, regret, and so forth.

I think you get the idea. Our hope is that by helping humanity, humans will find more love in all aspects of their lives.

In our service, which is borne of love, we have been evident on Earth in countless ways. We've pushed handcarts through the snow, reminded babies to breathe at their birth, and helped the blind to find other ways to see and inspire others. We have been known to give profound messages or whisper in an ear the words that changed a nation. We have assisted people in most dire situations. We have inspired writers and artists to create masterpieces.

Children know we are around. They see us, play with us, and even call us by name. Adults sometimes refer to us as their imaginary friends. It is confusing to children when adults tell them we do not exist, because we are as real to children as their parents are.

Even though many humans have completely forgotten us or choose not to acknowledge their sense of us, bringing us into your life is quite simple. By listening with your heart, you will know we are there. Ask for a sign, and we may touch your hair, caress your shoulder, or warm your heart. You may hear us in music as we sing along. You may even be able to see us or hear us whisper in your ear.

We have been heard in many minds and hearts. We have been seen and witnessed by many. Our stories are told in writings created throughout the ages. We have been a part of miracles. We inspire and build. We share love and give of peace. We rejoice in your successes, give encouragement through the tough times, and are with you even when you believe that you are completely alone.

We are there for births, deaths, and every human experience in between. At least one of us is always with you no matter what.

We have many ways of letting you know that we are around. I especially like to use music, the lyrics of certain songs on the radio, or a message on television. Sometimes I have caused a book to drop from a shelf or created vivid scenes in dreams. For example, you will know we are around when you hear the Lullaby.

How I acquired this responsibility was quite simple. There was a wonderful spirit, just barely out of creation. I had an attraction to its energy, and I knew it was the one for me to be with. I knew that, together, we would make a great team. I was given the chance to serve this spirit throughout every experience, in every lifetime, in every world.

This particular spirit is very special, and I have been very blessed to help it grow and progress. It is my responsibility to be with that soul, to help protect and comfort and love it unconditionally. I, along with the other angels that come and go from its life, ensure that it encounters other spirits and situations in order for it to grow. (All of this occurs according to a predetermined plan each time an incarnation is anticipated. Soon you will learn how this is done.)

From the very beginning, created from a spark of the Creator, this soul glowed brightly. A sweet, tender being with a thirst to learn, she has since been patient with the process of growing and always has a sense of peace around her. This was a very good start for a soul, and I felt that she and I could work very well together.

She has chosen to be called Sarah on Earth this time. She likes the vibration of the name, and it reminds her of a previous life, a few centuries ago, which she spent as a Sarah in Jerusalem. She remembers all of her past lives now, but soon she will not be able to remember any of them.

In a way, it is good that Sarah will forget her other lives and the lessons she learned during them. Because of this, she will not be influenced by what she was like or by people and situations she encountered previously. She will have the opportunity to create herself and her life experiences using free will and start her life on Earth with a relatively clean slate. Sarah will have some residual knowledge and memories, but she will forget Who She Is. This is where I, and a host of others she has employed, will step in. We will assist her in creating as much of the preplanned situations and life events that Sarah wants in order for her to get the most soul growth possible.

Oh, Sarah has picked some tough challenges in the past. She wanted to learn humility, so she incarnated as a stable hand for a tyrant knight. When she wanted to learn about greed, her soul became an unscrupulous banker who stole money from everyone. The banker was eventually stoned to death.

Sarah chose to arrive again on October eleventh. This date was not chosen randomly. Sarah picked it out very carefully, with those who would be her parents, among others. She conferred with the Agency. Together, they studied the stars and planets, the gridlines, the Mayan calendar, and many other sources. In the next chapter, we will take a peek as Sarah discusses some of the details of her upcoming life with these important players, and as you will see, neither her life nor any life on Earth is accidental.

Sarah and I have been through quite a lot, as you can imagine. It has been rewarding to know her, to see her grow, and to be able to guide her and comfort her through many lifetimes. I love my job serving Sarah, and I love Sarah with every part of me. It's a joy to be her guide, her angel, and her friend.

It's What I'm Here For

I'm by your side
I've got your back
And if it's courage
That you lack
I'll pick you up
And help you through
You've got to know
I'm here for you

I love you now
I always will
Love never ends
Though time stands still
You can always count on me
And I will listen to your plea

Just call on me
I'm as close as I can be
Call on me
Call on me
I'm as close as I can be
And it's what I'm here for

No purer love you'll ever know
Remember this from long ago
I'm always here
To give you strength
Do what I can
To any length

Just call on me
I'm as close as I can be
Call on me
Call on me
I'm as close as I can be
And it's what I'm here for

CHAPTER 2
MY FAVORITE PEOPLE
AND PLACES

Sarah

I'm known as Sarah now. That will be my name when I incarnate again. I know I am going back to Earth, because I feel the urge to go. It is up to me to make that choice. I'm getting myself ready; I can tell. It's not like I haven't done this before.

My soul has matured through hundreds of incarnations. My most recent life ended in 1947, and I happily returned here. I started going to Earth when there was hardly any language spoken at all. That was very challenging, but the lessons were simple ones like surviving, sharing, learning to be part of a tribe, stuff like that.

If you would like to compare the maturity or age of my soul to that on Earth, I'd be an average teenager, about sixteen years old. We don't measure years here, or time for that matter. We do, however, feel the desire to grow and mature in spiritual ways by living lives on Earth. By learning the lessons we choose while incarnated, we can advance and become Guardian angels if we want. I think that's what I'd like to do eventually.

On Earth, I've been a soldier (actually several different soldiers in many wars in places all over the planet), a sailor, a farmer, a farmer's wife, an African child (I starved to death), a slave, a nurse in the Crimean war, and in my last life a beggar in India.

I like being on Earth. Well, most of the time. What I don't like is forgetting almost everything that I've already learned. I understand that it has to be that way or I would probably just cruise through lives without even trying to learn the lessons. I know once I cross over into the spirit world again that I'm the one who decides how much I learned, how I did, and so on. It's good not to be judged by others because I think that would make it hard. I have Areanna to talk to about all of this, and my soul family, of course.

Areanna is amazing, and I love her so much. She loves me as much or more. I can't remember not having her with me, and she does everything she can to help me in every incarnation. I know that she can't do everything for me (Or what would be the point?), but she gives me hints and helps along the way.

Areanna isn't the only one helping me through these lives. I have my soul family. Most of them have been with me for as long as I can remember, as well. We all work together to be a part of one another's Earth lives to set up situations to teach us the lessons we want to learn. For example, in my last life, Seth played the role of the person who would steal anything I had, including clothing and food. I asked him to do this for me before we incarnated so that I could learn to trust that my needs would be taken care of and that I could rely on the goodness of strangers for help. The funny thing is, I was the beggar that would get handouts from Emily (another soul family member), who wanted to learn about sharing her wealth. She was proud in that life, wearing gold jewelry and fine silk. One day, she recognized me as a soul family member when she really looked into my eyes, and then she gave me a little money. Her husband (who happened to be Ethan) would punish her if he caught her. Ethan's lesson was about controlling his temper.

So, you see, our existences intertwine. We help one another through our lessons, then, once we all arrive back here, we talk about how well we did with our roles. We love each other very much or else we wouldn't be able to do this. But it doesn't always have to be tough. Though sometimes on Earth we have been very cruel to one another, at other times, we have chosen to marry and have families and live wonderful lives.

I am enjoying my time off and the beautiful place I've imagined and created here. Let me tell you about my favorite places.

Because I enjoy gardens and growing things, I (with Areanna's help) have created a garden where anything and everything can grow. Nothing can die here, so my gardening skills cannot really be tested (thank goodness). There is an endless variety of flowers, ferns, and trees. Food isn't required as sustenance, but that doesn't mean there aren't fruits and vegetables. The taste and texture of each are more exquisite than you can imagine. We can eat what we want and how much we want without any worries.

The colors of every plant in the garden are brilliant, filled with a light that glows from within each kind. The range of hues is endless, with shades that defy anything Earthly. Each growing thing contains a soul of its own, a substance of light and love that brings joy to the beholder.

The fragrances that come from the flowers are sometimes sweet, and sometimes spicy and pungent, but they always bring with them an emotion of peace or joy or love. There are scents on Earth that do that to a certain degree, but here, everything is so much more intense.

I love butterflies, so my garden is filled with them. Oh, yes, and dragonflies, too. They have various colors, and I am able to talk to them with my mind. They let me catch them and play with them. There's a wide variety of birds as well. I don't have many insects in my garden, and I made sure that I do not have any spiders. Since I had such a bad experience with them once, I don't want them around. I love to explore, so I enjoy my long hiking paths, along which I can play with many different animals.

Not far from the garden, just a thought away really, is a waterfall. You have similar ones on Earth in the jungles of Hawaii. This waterfall can sing. I could sit next to it forever and be perfectly happy, listening to the beautiful sounds it makes and the messages of the songs. The water that falls changes colors and feels wonderful to the touch. I enjoy swimming in the pool at the bottom of the falls. On Earth I have not been able to master swimming very well, but here, I swim perfectly.

In my favorite places, I can imagine storms, the gentle rainfall that freshens everything. I enjoy the sprinkling of tiny crystals. It is really something to see. My storms don't involve thunder. Some of my friends like thunder, but it reminds me too much of sounds from the battlefield.

I have another place I love to go and that is through space. I can travel with the speed of a thought, darting through meteor showers, zipping through galaxies, and getting close to the stars. I've visited many planets and find each one fascinating. The Earth's sun is especially fun to watch because of the churning gasses and the shooting flares.

Any spirit here can have whatever kind of surroundings it creates. It is easy to see differences among their personalities. I really like to visit my soul family members, because not one of their places is the same.

I've come to know their Guardian angels as well. They have different dispositions and ideas, so it keeps things interesting. It isn't unusual to have our angels work together to help all of us in our lessons. Sometimes we don't even realize what they are doing and how they are influencing us. I think it's a good thing that we aren't aware of them all the time on Earth. I like to feel like I'm never alone, but I also like to feel somewhat independent, like I'm understanding, learning, and accomplishing some things on my own. I guess I still have a pride issue to overcome, don't I?

CHAPTER 3
MORE ABOUT THE LULLABY

Music is well said to be the speech of angels; in fact,
nothing among the utterances allowed to man is felt
to be so divine. It brings us near to the infinite.

—Thomas Carlyle (1795–1881)

Areanna

The Lullaby gives a clear direction and purpose to life. Its vibration reminds you that love is all there is, all that matters, all that is "required" or requested, and the only thing that gives sense to life and living, to lessons and growth. When you hear it, you receive the message that you are on the right track.

On Earth, it is easy to become so distracted by the lessons that you are unable to experience the Lullaby, even just a little bit. Conversely, a soul is accustomed to having the Lullaby here in the spirit world. It is all around and through all. The Lullaby is love, manifesting itself through tones and notes and song, the vibration of the Universe that traverses space and time. The soul can experience every nuance. In fact, because the Lullaby is so prevalent here, the soul can begin to tune it out, becoming deaf to it in the same way humans cannot hear white noise after a time.

We angels must remind souls before they incarnate to focus on the Lullaby again, to take with them every remembrance they can about it, because it is an essential tool on Earth.

The Lullaby is a part of all, of the basic form and substance of everything in creation. In human form, it can be found connected to DNA, to the cell. Any object ever created, any animal that has walked the Earth, any plant that has grown has had the Lullaby as part of its essence. Animals and creatures are more in touch with the vibration, with the oneness of All That Is. In everything that experiences the vibration, even in the objects you call inanimate, there is a response. All things are undeniably affected in a positive, loving way.

Let me explain it another way. The Lullaby causes vibration at a very specific frequency and can be felt and heard by anything that is in tune to that particular vibration. Many objects, such as crystals, vibrate at frequencies that assist with healing. Because the Earth is crystalline-based, it responds to the vibrations and energy of the Lullaby in a way that benefits human beings.

When the soul incarnates, it assumes normal hearing, but because there is so much chaos and fear on the Earthly plane, the Lullaby is drowned out. The oneness in spirit is forgotten at birth when the soul travels through a veil on amnesia. Though a kind of dust or essence from the spirit world may be brought through the veil, this is rare. When it happens, the soul is more likely to remember and be in tune with the spiritual realm.

Young ones coming to Earth at this time can remember more of the Lullaby than ever before. They have been labeled Crystal children and are gifted ones, incarnated with special insight and abilities. If allowed to grow into Who They Are, they bring the world special messages and can help humanity. They expound their truth if given the opportunity. It is unfortunate that many of them are told that they are mistaken, that they are strange and are looked down upon. Their gifts could be lost or buried if not nurtured.

There are also souls that incarnate who know the Lullaby to perfection, but, because of the lives they chose, are not able to express to the world what they know. If you look deep into the eyes of someone who is mentally challenged or autistic, you will see true love and peace. They did not return to Earth to learn lessons for their own soul growth. They returned in a particular way so that others would learn their lessons. These special spirits may be unable to express love verbally, but their essences carry the Lullaby. They are wonderful teachers.

Those souls who have chosen to pursue life lessons that require them to be purposefully cruel to others know they may never hear the Lullaby while incarnated. But they also understand that if they can learn their lessons and rise above, they will eventually hear and feel the Lullaby again, because the essence of Who They Are becoming cannot deny the power and beauty of the Lullaby.

Any soul can hear the Lullaby in quiet, peaceful moments, but finding such moments can prove to be difficult, especially if the soul is surrounded by negativity. And if the predominant emotion there is fear or anger, the Lullaby cannot be experienced at all, except by individuals who have spent their entire lives focusing on it.

Sometimes there are adult souls that remember the Lullaby and will hum or sing it to a child. Usually the soothing tones will comfort the child as the child remembers it. Souls do not want to forget the Lullaby, and because of this, they naturally seek places, events, and people that remind them of home.

After time, as souls gain more experience while incarnated, they may hear the Lullaby as they drift off to sleep or awake. Awareness comes in many forms, such as shivers or goose bumps, an "ah-ha" moment, a knowing, déjà vu feeling, a moment when hair stands on end, or a warm sensation in the heart.

And some souls, even when they finally hear the Lullaby, enjoy it only briefly, believing they are hearing things that don't exist. They may become worried that if they share what they are hearing and experiencing, others will think they are crazy. Fear plays into it again, keeping the Lullaby from being fully perceived.

Many individuals seek the Lullaby in churches or in religion. These organizations have their hymns, chants, and gospel songs. These songs can be very inspiring and beautiful, but none reach the perfection of the Lullaby.

The truth is, experiencing the Lullaby in nature can be easy and simple. Just listen. It is in the breeze, in a bird's song, even in the sound of falling snow. It is in the sound of a seed as it opens to let the sprout find the light. It can also be as loud as thunder or the pounding of waves on the shore in a storm, but most people won't hear it there.

Trying to find the Lullaby outside of yourself, however, is

missing the point, for it is in you. Yes, indeed, you wonderful, amazing being! The Lullaby is in you. It's in your nose so that you can smell fresh-baked bread. It's in your muscles so that you can move and play. It's in your bones so that you can stand tall. It's in your nervous system so that its messages can be communicated throughout your body. And it is especially in your heart. The Lullaby reaches into the energy of your heart, causing a sense of peace and love.

Seek and find the Lullaby within. Just breathe slowly and deeply, and feel its energy fill you. Close your eyes and feel your heart beating. Sense your fingertips and your feet as they connect with the Earth. Then know that all you are, every part of you, is connected with All That Is and that the Lullaby is with you and in you.

CHAPTER 4
LET'S TALK ABOUT GOING AGAIN

Areanna

Making the decision to return to Earth is a process that starts with discussion—a simple conversation between the spirit being and its Guardian angel that may include other soul family members and their angels as well.

Sarah, as she mentioned before, has been thinking about going back to "school." Her soul has been here for a while. She has processed her most recent life on Earth and now feels the urge to return and learn more.

I do not ever push Sarah to go. This must be a decision she makes on her own. Each time she approaches the subject, I listen and give her my opinion as a trusted friend and confidant. I ultimately want what is best for her and will advise her accordingly.

Because we are at the waterfall so often, that was where we were when she most recently spoke to me about returning. Here's how the conversation went:

Sarah: Areanna, I've been thinking that I want to go back to Earth. I've been considering it for a while. I have this yearning feeling, like the time is right again. What do you think?

Areanna: I've been waiting for you to make up your mind. You know that I will never push you in any way. It must be your decision. I love you no matter what. I always have.

Sarah: I love you, too. It's good to be able to talk to you about this. Okay. Well, I suppose we could talk about the lesson I could pick this time. Do you have any ideas?

Areanna: It isn't up to me. You want an idea? How about a lesson in pain? That has been a powerful lesson for you through several lives. You are getting much better at not complaining, focusing on something other than the pain, and not becoming bitter and lashing out at those around you.

Sarah: Pain. Well, I don't think you really understand how difficult that lesson is since you've never had a body. I realize that pain is part of having a human body, but I really don't want it to be the main lesson again. Not right now. Let's think of something else. What about strength?

Areanna: What kind of strength are you talking about? Physical, emotional, mental? There are so many aspects to it. It will help if you can be more specific.

Sarah: Strength of character or strength … physical strength. Hum. I was pretty strong in the life when I wrestled bears in the circus in Russia. But that life wasn't specifically about strength as much as about communicating with animals. I really enjoyed being able to look into a creature's eyes and know that they understood what I wanted them to do and how I felt. Animals are amazing when it comes to sensing emotions. Getting back to strength …

Areanna: Being mentally strong could be interesting. Withstanding torture while staying centered and focused, not giving into pain. That is a difficult lesson, and there are plenty of opportunities for it on Earth right now. Human beings have not evolved to the point of knowing that torture has nothing to do with love, which is what their souls desire to learn.

Sarah: Oh, I have been on both sides, being tortured and torturing others. Neither side was pleasant from the soul's perspective. But lessons are lessons, no matter what. Still, I think I'll pass on that one.

Areanna: There are so many lessons to choose from. If we made a list, it would be endless. Maybe we could talk about some of your past life lessons that you feel you could learn more from.

Sarah: Well, if we start with the first incarnation and work forward, that could be interesting. We usually just review a few incarnations and do not go back any farther.

Areanna: The first hundred lives really dealt with survival, being connected to the Earth in a way that helped you to find food, learning tribal dynamics, that sort of thing. I believe that you learned much from the time you broke both feet while hunting for food for your family and everyone starved to death.

Sarah: Getting the soul family involved with that one was interesting. What if we focus on chakras and lessons that have to do with them? Prosperity is a root chakra issue. I was a rich aristocrat once. I remember that I didn't treat people very well and didn't share my wealth, though I had every intention of giving money to the poor. My soul family suffered because I didn't share with them, but they grew immensely from the experience.

Areanna: It doesn't sound like you feel much remorse for that decision not to share your wealth. You have made good progress in regard to guilt. Since souls are the only ones to judge themselves, sometimes it is difficult for them to let go of the guilt. I have witnessed many of your soul family go through anguish after returning here because of the things they did on Earth. They forgot what the big picture is: that there is no judgment; there is only love.

Sarah: Oh, you know that I beat myself up sometimes. I think that is natural for the young soul.

Areanna: Yes, that's true. You are doing better through each incarnation, however.

Sarah: I don't think I want to live this next life dealing with a great deal of money. There are so many aspects to it: greed, envy, sharing, lack, abundance, worry, manifesting, guilt. Many souls will eventually learn that the love of it is not the root of all evil as some on Earth believe when they read it in the Bible or hear it from religious leaders. Money itself is just an object. Using money is an energy exchange. I'm glad I figured that part out. Regardless, I don't think I want to learn about another aspect of money this time around.

Areanna: Okay. Any other ideas?

Sarah: Maybe the lesson could be something about being

empowered. Many have called Earth a man's world, with most countries and major companies and religions being led by men. What if I was a strong woman and showed others that a woman can be strong and a great leader without giving up the feminine side of being human?

Areanna: That could be interesting. There certainly is an imbalance of that energy. The Earth has many lessons regarding duality.

Our conversation continued, covering many more topics, such as lessons resulting from lack of health, taking on other people's problems as your own, ego, violence, and addictions. Finally, we came to a conclusion when Sarah made a decision that felt like the right one. The next step was to get cooperation from Sarah's soul family and to plan what parts each one would play.

Sarah: This is great! I truly believe that my soul family has my best interest and growth at heart, so I think that they'll want to work with me. I'll let them all know my decision right away, and we'll start working through the details.

Areanna: Yes, your soul family has wonderful members that you have worked with in so many lifetimes. But before you speak to them, let's make a decision regarding your birthday, astrological sign, and name, since these aspects will influence your personality, which will also affect how you approach your lesson.

Sarah: Oh, of course. Well, I think that balance and fairness could be useful, no matter what the lesson. What do you think about a birthday within the days of Libra?

Areanna: I think that will work very well.

Sarah: I'd like to be somewhat adventuresome this time. Do you know which Life Path Number relates to that aspect of the personality?

Areanna: Yes, that would be a Five. If you choose October eleventh of the upcoming cycle of years, that would give you a Five Life Path Number.

Sarah: That sounds good to me. And I want to be called Sarah Jo Neal. I like the sound of it.

Areanna: I will meet with the Agency and let them know of your decision so they may study the planets, grid lines, Earthly calendars, and other tools to make sure that all will be in place for you to have the optimum opportunity to complete your lesson.

Sarah: You are so wonderful, Areanna. Thank you so much for everything that you do. I know that I could not do this without you, and I'm so happy that I will never know what it would be like not to have an angel with me.

Areanna: You are always welcome, Sarah. It is my joy and duty.

On the Ride

I think that I'll go back again
Back to the Earth I love
Try a new life just for me
And with help from up above
Been wondering what to do this time
That I haven't tried before
What lesson would be the one for me?
What could this life have in store?

For this old soul
Getting back in the saddle
For this old soul
Getting back on the ride
Will be like slipping on a glove
In a form that I will love

For this old soul
I'm getting back in the saddle
For this old soul
I'm getting back on the ride
Getting back in the saddle
Getting back on the ride

Should I be a famous lawyer?
A singer extraordinaire?
Be a chef or sit around all day?
Spend life as a monk in prayer?
What lesson should I pursue?
Should I learn about hope and fear?

What about a life of crime?
What would be the best, my dear?

Lust, gluttony, greed, sloth, wrath, envy, and pride
These are all lessons that I've tried
Haven't mastered everything, oh no
But I'm game for all that life can bring

CHAPTER 5
LET THE PLANNING BEGIN

Areanna

It takes a great deal of work to orchestrate a soul's reappearance in the physical world on Earth. Oh, I don't know if I can even do it justice, but I will try my best to help you understand and appreciate what occurs.

First, there is the soul itself, this beautiful, shiny, brilliant light that holds intelligence, potential, and love. This soul, after being created so very long ago, goes through much learning and growing before incarnating upon the Earth. That entrance is somewhat like going to school. The more advanced souls and others help in every way, giving the best of themselves to the entering soul in order to guide it to greater understanding.

After several incarnations and a certain amount of learning has occurred, the soul, along with its own personal guides, decides what aspect of enlightenment would be beneficial the next time around. Sarah and I have accomplished this as described to you previously.

The Agency has been in on all aspects of the planning. It is their responsibility to assure that the world, planets, and stars will be aligned and energies and vibrations in proper balance during the major events the soul has planned so that the soul will have the optimal benefits to complete its journey and lessons. The Agency has the overall picture of life experience of all individual souls on Earth, including the animal and plant kingdoms.

As angel guides and Guardians, we are part of all aspects of planning as well. We meet together to coordinate our involvement when our charges are interacting with each other. We influence their lives more than they realize, especially since they have forgotten much (and sometimes all) of what they know here in spirit.

After that point in the process, the real work begins. It takes many situations and individuals to cause the life lessons to play out. Many must agree to assist in whatever capacity they are able to cause the experiences that the soul is asking for, and not all of these experiences are pleasant, because the soul cannot grow without opposition and challenge. Certain soul family members may agree to be the "bad guy" in certain lessons. But free will, the power to make choices, is a base component for everyone.

Situations are coordinated, probabilities are calculated, and a Possibilities Board is created. The Board is an amazing object that assists everyone to move a likeness of themselves on a mock Earth, tracking their actions and choices. It appears in the center of the souls who are working with it as they discuss their upcoming lives. It is similar to a board game on Earth. The key souls meet together many times with the Possibilities Board, working out the overall strategy, and then ultimately the details. I will describe the Board in greater detail when Sarah and her soul family gather to use it. The main goal in all of this is to assist the soul in its growth by giving it the opportunity to learn its chosen lessons.

Although the lessons themselves are very important, the most important goal— through both the planning and the subsequent incarnation on Earth—is love. How much love did the soul give to others? How did it express love? These are question we ask once the incarnation is over.

When a soul realizes this goal while incarnated, it makes everything much easier, simpler, and more joyful. One of the hardest parts of such an endeavor, however, is the soul learning to love itself. That lesson is one that many souls choose to repeat, as it is usually not mastered in just one lifetime.

Loving yourself attracts more love, and it does so in wondrous ways. This phenomenon is what your world calls the Law of Attraction.

Once the soul has everyone in place, each individual involved waits for the proper time to step into the physical body it will occupy. The soul is allowed to inspect each of these physical bodies while they are developing and growing, to ensure that each body is physically capable to meet the prearranged goal that the soul wants. If the body can't handle what the soul needs, there may be a delay in the process while a new one is created. By the time of the entrance, all is in perfect order, although sometimes for humans, it does not all appear to be.

The entrance is a momentous occasion. The soul, accompanied by many guides, soul family members, and others gather where the emergence takes place. Many of the soul family are already physically present on Earth, ready to start playing their parts.

I have been a witness to hundreds of these events. Many deliveries happen in hospitals, but there have been other settings. I have seen births on the plains, in deserts, on mountains, and in caves. The event has occurred in cars, on airplanes, and in boats, as well as in all types of houses and in about every room of a house that you can imagine. Sarah has experienced all of these types of births and more.

Reincarnation

Jumping in with two feet
We'll be running down the street
Before you know it
Happy for my life to start
I know the game by heart
I'm gonna flow with it

Bring no memories of the past
Those lives went by so fast
Time's just an illusion
As I play with my soul mates
New times we will create
With a little confusion

It's time to start again
Reconnect with my old friends
Reincarnation
When I get a look at you
We'll have a sense of déjà vu
Reincarnation

Get ready, world
I'm coming back again
Got a new life starting
Be ready, world
For a brand new me
With a little history
And this time I'll get it right
Cause I've got a new life starting

We're gonna dance the dance
We'll take another chance
To get it right this time around
To act out our parts
And listen with our hearts
That's the best place to start

Feeling better and brighter
My heart's feeling lighter
Happy as it's ever been before
Cause I know for sure
That I'm gonna get it right
I'm gonna shine my light
I'm gonna get it right

CHAPTER 6
GETTING THE SOUL FAMILY ON BOARD

Areanna

The place we meet has no walls; only energy is a boundary. The round expanse is filled with light that comes from all directions, as well as from the angels that line the perimeter. Their role is to witness and support the process, as well as to advise on questions and concerns that may arise.

The space also has a feeling of contracting and expanding as souls and angels enter, their energy separating at first, then blending with the others'. Soul family members have the ability to become one with each other, according to their desires, yet they remain separate according to their own individual preferences, as free will is basic to the soul.

Separateness is an interesting concept. The Earth plane provides the perfect stage for its illusion. When a soul is on Earth, there is a feeling of being separate, yet the spirit knows and understands fully that there is no separation, that everyone and everything is connected. And depending on the state of awareness or consciousness of the soul, it has the ability to dissolve its own feelings of separateness. During dream states, in particular, the soul can experience a bright remembrance of being one with all, as it is here, always. Here, there is only being and oneness.

This particular soul family has these sessions many times as one or all the members participate in each other's incarnations. This initial meeting lays the groundwork for all others.

Each angel has a different appearance, different energy that gives the impression of female, male, or a mixture of both. The love that shines from them has various colors, like gold glitter or variegated threads swirling, a tangible silky mist.

Sarah chose the decor for the room, the atmosphere and ambience for this event. Her themes in previous times have been around Earthly nature scenes, such as spacious Japanese gardens, beach scenes from Polynesia, and the majestic mountains of Colorado. Each one has been a reminder of a particular lifetime Sarah enjoyed. Now everyone is enjoying the soft, melodious sounds of the Lullaby, along with the songbirds. She particularly loves the meadowlark, the Indigo Bunting, and the skylark. To add another dimension, Sarah has included the scent of roses and gardenias, her favorite flowers.

Sarah's soul family arrives with their angels. Greetings are filled with love and joy. Everyone shines with an inner light as well. Because these particular souls have been working with each other closely throughout many incarnations, their appearance has begun to take on a similar colored hue. It is just one of the many things that shows connectedness between souls on this side of the veil.

Conversation occurs as quickly as thought. I will expand the dialogue, however, as if it were occurring on Earth, with each individual speaking in turn.

"This is so 'Sarah.'" Beth was the first to arrive. She has been Sarah's child, teacher, and best friend. They are very close and have not incarnated without the other participating. "The butterflies are a nice touch."

"I'd rather see hawks and owls," Joe replies. Joe prefers a masculine role to Sarah's predominantly female appearances. He has been her brother, husband, and father many times. "Remember when we all went as Mongolian nomads and chased those crazy sheep?"

"Oh, yeah," says Seth. "I remember. You were pretty good with the horses. I got to take care of the lambs. That was fun. I did end up with a nasty wound in my back when invaders came to steal the flock and killed me. I have carried that mark through many incarnations as a reminder of that hard but satisfying life." Seth looks around the room. "You know, Sarah won't go anywhere on Earth where there aren't butterflies. No cold climates, that sort of thing. Where do you think she wants to go this time?" Seth enjoys the same type of Earth climate and atmosphere as Sarah. After freezing to death in Montana in one life and dying of dehydration in the Sahara desert in another, he now prefers to incarnate in temperate climates.

"I don't know," Emily says. "I have to admit, I'm glad that she's decided to go to Earth again. I like it there most of the time."

Emily has always been the adventurous one, living at various times as a nomad, a soldier of fortune, and a mountain man. Now she has chosen to learn about more feminine roles. "Maybe we'll be mountain climbers or deep sea explorers. That would be exciting."

"*Namaste*, everyone." Nathan arrives, along with his angel Teharajon. Nathan always planned incarnations that were difficult, leading him to deep soul searching. At times, he has felt unsuccessful in fulfilling his goals; however, his most recent lessons—those learned from being a teacher, a nun to orphaned children, and a mother of thirteen, for example—have brought him much more fulfillment.

"Hey, Nathan," says Beth. "Are you ready to do this again?"

"Sure. I've got some ideas for my lessons. Teharajon and I have worked out some signals and signs that we are going to use this time. I want to stay on the path as much as possible. It can be tough remembering what we are there for, without some signs and help along the way," Nathan explains.

"Yes, and thanks to our angels," Beth says quietly and with much respect. "It would be much harder without them." She gives her angel Mesha a knowing, loving look.

There is a chorus of agreement.

"Of course."

"Thanks."

"We love you."

The angels in attendance send a subliminal message to the group. "It is our job and our joy. Serving you is what we do. We are here for you and want you to succeed."

Seth joins in. "I remember many lives when I didn't rely on or even remember I had angels to help. Now I make sure that Ciaramai and I also have signals to remind me. I've missed those signals plenty of times, though. Too bad at the time, I suppose, but I learned from it. I guess that's the point, isn't it? Learning. Have you noticed how we have changed?"

Everyone looks around, smiling and sending out love, expressing appreciation for their growth and knowledge as well as for the bond they share as a family.

Joe replies. "Yes, but I still feel like I have a long way to go as a soul. It's good that we can take it as fast or as slow as we want, that this isn't a race, you know?"

"Where's David?" Emily asks the group. "Isn't he going to be here?"

"Not this time," replies Joe.

Everyone nods in understanding and sends their love and support to David. Being as close as a thought away, he acknowledges them and returns his love to them. They understand perfectly why he has decided not to be a part of Sarah's upcoming life. There is no judgment, and they respect him for Who He Is and what he has accomplished.

Suddenly, there is a change in the energy of the space, a brightening of the light and a slight change in the tempo of The Lullaby. Sarah has arrived.

As she enters, Sarah clears her thoughts and focuses on what she feels and wishes to express to her family. Acknowledgment filters through as those present begin to sense what Sarah is projecting.

She addresses her soul family with the knowledge that they all love and support her. "I want to thank all of you for coming to this initial planning session for my next incarnation. All of you have played significant roles in my past lives. I wouldn't be where I am as a soul now if each of you hadn't been there for me."

There is a chorus of support.

"Oh, Sarah, don't worry."

"We are here for you."

"It's fine. We are glad to do it."

Sarah resumes. "I am ready to do this. Areanna and I have discussed many options for my primary lesson, which each of you are beginning to understand now. Is everyone able to pick up on it? I am very excited and positive about this decision."

"Good for you."

"That's awesome."

"Very good choice."

Sarah adds, "I also want to overcome some fears I've had over many lives—my fear of spiders and thunder. I've dealt with these fears over and over, but I want to overcome them once and for all."

Beth directs her thoughts to me. "With her main lesson, as well as these, isn't that too much for one lifetime?"

My reply is, "If Sarah does not believe so, then anything can be accomplished. That is where all of us come in. As long as we do our parts and do not forget, Sarah will be able to overcome her fears."

Sarah adds, "These fears have troubled me and stopped me from doing things in so many past lives. Remember when I was going to study the weather, become an expert in cloud formation? But I couldn't get past the noise of thunder. Too many battles, too many explosions. And don't even get me started on the spider thing! Being tortured with them when I was in Africa has had a lot of lingering effects on me. I don't want them to get the best of me again!"

"We are behind you," Seth states in a sentiment held by all. "Now, what do you want us to do?"

"What would you like me to be?" asks Beth.

"You have been so many things for me," Sarah says. "I'd like you to be my mother in this next life. Would you do that for me?"

"Of course, I'll be happy to," Beth replies.

"Joe, would you be my father again?" Sarah asks.

"Anything you say, Sarah. Beth and I can work out the details of the lessons we want to have together as a couple. These will affect you, too, since you'll be our daughter. I don't want to have to work very hard on soul growth this time, though. I am kind of burned-out and feel like I want an extended rest, but I'll go back for you. We can talk about this more when we use the Possibilities Board in our next session."

"Okay, Joe. We can work together on that. Thanks for doing this for me," Sarah says.

Sarah continues to give her soul family basic instructions, telling them her wishes for their respective roles. They all realize how important soul lessons are and are very cooperative. They all realize there is no judgment on anyone if a lesson is not completed fully or is changed from the original plan. They all trust that each soul among them will do its best.

Going Back to Earth Again

Going back to Earth again
        Yes, you are
Going back to school, and then
        You'll go far
I'll see life there in a different way
Plan to give love every day
        Don't forget to give love every day
Yes, I will

Will meet up with my friends down there
        Yes, you will
Gonna learn to really care
        Yes, you will
Will tell everyone that I see
I'm working on the improved me
        And we'll be there to help you, you'll see
Yes, you will

We're happy to be connected
We've done this many times
It's a joy, and we're committed
To help our souls learn
        And grow
And serve
        And more

Won't be long now, plans are coming together
        Yes, indeed
You're with me no matter what the weather

For every need
Have to pack my bags super light
    I hope your memory of home burns bright
My family will help to make things go right
    Yes, we will

I'll make it through every day
I'll remember Who I Am
I thank you for the parts you play
And I won't be getting a final exam

CHAPTER 7
BEHIND THE SCENES

Areanna

When a soul returns to Earth, it crosses through what has been described as a veil. The veil is not a physical piece of cloth, of course, but a curtain of energy that causes the soul to begin forgetting both the plans it made with others and the lessons it wants to accomplish. The soul has to forget in order to go through the experiences that cause it to learn and grow. There would be no point to incarnation if the plan remained crystal clear. Still, for some, memories of the spirit world, the angel guides, and certain gifts of the spirit are carried well into the physical life.

There is a great deal of the Earth experience that human beings are not aware of, things happening behind the scenes. Even in the spirit world, souls are not fully conscious of the influence that angels and other entities have, which is necessary to ensure the incarnated soul receives the experiences it planned.

For instance, we Guardian angels have continual direct contact with the souls we are entrusted with. Some humans are aware of our presence and even our messages, but most are not. In that way, we are able to influence and guide without disruption.

Free will is essential and part of the global plan for the Earth experience. It cannot be altered for any reason. As a soul makes a decision, even a simple one, we angels may exercise influence over it by placing an idea in the mind or staging a problem for the soul to encounter. We are there to give the soul the optimal opportunity to succeed. This does not mean that everyone heeds the signs or hears us, however.

Though many have forgotten we are with them, or see but do not recognize as divine our essence or our actions, they call upon us often. We find it amusing that often when a person asks for a miracle and we perform it, the human then discards it as chance.

In those instances when we have answered the same request repeatedly and, repeatedly, the soul purposely ignores the signs it receives, the soul loses its ability to sense our signals and voices. Though we may try in many different ways to get our message through so that the soul will recognize it, each time the soul discards it, the person may become more resistant to future signs. It is as if the individual has created a wall, decreasing the ability to acknowledge or perceive messages. This can lead to increased difficulties for the soul.

Still, we Guardian angels do not stop sending our messages. We are always there to assist, to love, and to serve through whatever may come. We hold no judgment, disappointment, anger, or frustration toward the person.

Many in the angelic realm have never incarnated. We who

have not, do not know what it is like to forget everything. We have perfect knowledge of everything that has occurred to the soul: the planning of lessons, the interactions with soul family members, the signs to use that bring recognition. We also do not know what it is like to have a physical body and so cannot relate to sensations related to the physical realm, such as being tired, having pain, aging, or being hungry.

The hierarchy of angels works together, depending on what is needed. Other angels and ascended masters have the specific skills required to accomplish certain tasks, so we may call upon any of them at any time based on their specialties, their influences, or their stewardships (guardianships).

For example, Sarah will be a Libra. Being born in the fall, in the time of harvest, she is under the order of AA Uriel. He helps those who are completing projects, providing them with the energy they may need to succeed. He then helps them recognize the fruits of their labors and the importance of sharing their bounty with others. A patron of music, AA Uriel can also award a soul the gift of creativity, if requested. And he can provide opportunities to turn bitter disappointment into great blessings.

Another Libra angel is Barbiel, whose main job is to help humankind be honest about what is good or not good. He assists individuals in facing the consequences of their choices, helping them acquire personal understanding through their experiences.

Angel Ihiazel is one who inspires artists and writers. He, like AA Uriel, blesses souls with creativity and imagination. Libras that work with him may be blessed with personalities that are gracious and charming.

For Sarah's current incarnation, her soul family angels and I have met. We assist one another throughout all of her and her soul family's incarnations. Together, we have also called upon the Guardian angels of other individuals—those not in the soul family—who appear and influence the lives of the souls we are entrusted with. As I have said, there is much that goes on.

CHAPTER 8
WON'T YOU COME
OUT AND PLAY?

Areanna

Even though Sarah could be there in less than a thought, she prefers to take the long way, through mountain trails and deep forests, around lakes and streams. This is the adventurous route, but one without the danger of wild animals and physical injury that could occur on Earth. There is a bright sun shining and a gentle breeze. Woodland creatures are in abundance, always knowing they are safe. The air is filled with the sound of birds and the scent of flowers and, of course, the sweet melody of the Lullaby.

"David?" Sarah tentatively speaks as she approaches his teepee. David has been here since the end of his last incarnation, preferring the seclusion to interacting with others. He has chosen a teepee to live in for many reasons, but mostly to remind him to honor Gaia by living simply and peacefully. David has learned how to live off of the lands of the Earth, using only what he needs and sharing much with his tribes. Through many incarnations, he has been a strong, wise leader and shaman, never begrudging the difficulties he has faced, remembering that he had asked for those experiences and had created his own lives. With David's goal of becoming an ascended master, he has faced each challenge with bravery. Love has been his guiding light in the last of his incarnations. Now he exists in virtual solitude, enjoying the company of only his Guardian angel Po and few others.

David finds joy and peace in writing. He was a published writer of poems once and found it very satisfying. He was not well-known but was well loved by those on Earth who knew him. They frequently sought out his company and wisdom.

Po and David coexist as beings practically equal in temperament and wisdom. They share all thoughts and all travels, often going to far-reaching stars and galaxies for the peace they find there. They have recently returned from the Cat's Eye Nebula, where they experienced a dying star firsthand.

David has always loved Sarah and has played many roles in her incarnations. He has been her lover, her friend, her murderer, her executioner, her brother, and her father. She has been his mistress, queen, and hunting companion.

"Yes, Sarah. Come in. I knew you were coming."

"Well, of course you did," Sarah says with a little laugh. She felt a great amount of love coming from the teepee before she even stepped in, knowing that the love they shared is unconditional. Now she smiles as she sees David seated on the floor in a lotus position. Memories of their lives together flood her heart.

David is what is referred to as an old soul. He has experienced more incarnations than anyone in Sarah's soul family, as well as many more lessons in each life. She looks into his eyes and sees into his heart, sensing peace with a small amount of weariness around the edges.

"I'm so glad to see you," he says. "I understand that you are on your way back to Earth, the ultimate place of duality." The timbre of his voice denotes a little sadness. He knows the difficulties soul growth can bring, the hardship and pain. David also realizes that a human experience is a powerful way for the soul to feel fulfilled. Growing as a soul has rewards beyond number. Sarah lets her excitement shine through. "Yes, I'm going back soon. Everything is coming together nicely. But I have a feeling that you are not going to join me this time. I thought I'd come by and put a little pressure on you. Is it going to work?"

David draws a big sigh. "No, dear one. I always have the desire to help you, but not in physical form this time. My last lifetime was very difficult, as you can imagine, and I don't know if I ever will go back. I hope you understand."

"Could you tell me more about how that life affected you, so I can understand? I have never been in a concentration camp. I've heard others speak of it, and it sounds very difficult on so many levels."

"I don't like to speak of it, but for you, I will." He winks. Then a faraway look consumes his face and he draws the energy of remembrance toward him. His demeanor takes on a sense of pain and sadness.

"I chose to be a Jew during a very dark time for Jews on the

Earth. I knew the lessons I would face, because I chose them carefully and I embraced them. I also took that life and time carefully, knowing that there may never be another time on Earth that that type of situation would occur. My hope, as it was for the other many souls that joined me, was that the experience would teach humanity to never let that happen again. The lessons I chose took my soul to its very limits and fully tested my resolve to love everyone, no matter what they did to me. I knew this would be difficult, and that is why I did not ask other soul family members to join me in this particular life. I hope you understand that."

"Of course," Sarah softly replies.

"Soon after I was incarnated, my Earth mother died from an infection. My father was nowhere to be found. I was placed in an orphanage and was not adopted until I was ten years old. But all of that was planned, of course.

"My years in the orphanage were spent keeping other children quiet so we would not be beaten. The younger ones were usually adopted first, and I continued to care for those who were not adopted. We were quite the group of boys. There were no girls. The younger girls had all been adopted, and the older ones had been taken to help rich wives.

"Eventually, I was adopted by a Jewish family in the bakery business and put into manual labor, carrying heavy sacks of flour from wagons to the bakery. Before I came to live with them, their biological son had done most of the physical work, but he had died the month before from tuberculosis. The father had been badly burned, and the pain from his scars prevented him from doing much. They generally treated me well and felt very strongly that I should continue in the Jewish religion and beliefs.

"The setting was perfect for my plan to get into a concentration camp. I was twenty-eight and never married. I preferred a solitary life, devoted to working hard and sharing my meager bounty with those less fortunate than myself. The climate in the city was changing, and the power of fear gripped my community as the treatment of Jews escalated.

"I did not feel the desire to hide from my destiny. Many did, but most were found. My neighbors and I were gathered in a large group and placed in a large truck. It was winter and very cold.

"We were taken to a concentration camp in Auschwitz. As you know, we suffered tremendously. I knew that to fulfill my lessons I would have to be brave and calm, choosing to love my captors rather than hate them. I also chose to help those around me and to be an example of tolerance and hope. This was not easy, as you may imagine. We were beaten often, only fed rotten food occasionally, and lived in very cold barracks. Eventually there was only the kindness of others to keep you going.

It is quite amazing how fearful people can be of death; they will go through anything just to stay alive. On this side of the veil, it is easy to speak of death, knowing that it brings your soul to a place of your own making, which can be the most wonderful place imaginable."

"Oh, I totally agree with you," Sarah replies. "If only more souls could understand or remember that while they are incarnated."

"I don't tell you these things to have you feel any sense of sorrow for the suffering I went through. You asked to understand more of what I endured and get a sense of why I am not choosing to go back to Earth this time with the soul family," David explains.

"Weren't you eventually taken to a gas chamber?" Sarah asks.

"I was skin and bones before that could even happen. But, even just before my death, I never stopped helping where I could. Sharing my food, giving my blanket away, even just holding hands with someone who was frightened, offering a smile and a hug when I could. My resolve was strong to give love. So, when I returned here, I told Po that I was ready to have a long vacation." David smiles. "I am not sorry to tell you no, I won't be going back this time, Sarah, *Animae Dimidium Meae,* Half My Soul. I'm going to be right here. Please know that my love and support will be with you always, though."

Sarah takes in a deep breath. "Oh, I will miss you very much. I do understand though, and I hope you'll be watching out for me from time to time."

"You can be sure of that," David says.

They share a heartfelt hug and look deeply into each other's eyes, sharing a strong connection and recognition of Who They Are.

"Dear one, I am with you always," he says. "You will be fine. Everything will be fine."

"Of course!" And with that, Sarah turns to leave.

Duality

Duality is the mentality
It's part of being there
Even when it feels unfair

Boy and girl
Black and white
Many colors in between

Good or bad
Happy or sad
You'll be kind or you'll be mean

Peace or war
Rich or poor
Learn to deal with what you're dealt

Beauty or beast
Famine or feast
All emotions will be felt

Fat or thin
Lose or win
Big or small
Short or tall

Sinner and saint
Gay and straight
Love and hate

Up and down
Smile or frown
Big cities or small towns

Love without fear
As you do here
And you'll be fine, my dear

Remember to rise above duality
And love

CHAPTER 9
PLOTTING POSSIBILITIES

Sarah

I am getting so excited now. This is my favorite part of preparing to go to Earth. Though we have all done this so many times for one another, each time it is a whole different situation, a whole different game. It all depends on who is going to be who and what the lessons are everyone wants to experience.

This is how it works. My soul family gets together to plot out our strategies. As you know, we have already agreed upon what each person's role will be. Beth has agreed to be my mother and Joe my father. They have worked together to plan their own relationship, the possibilities of how they could meet, fall in love, plan their family, and so on. They each have specific things they want to accomplish on Earth as well, so they will need to coordinate their personal lessons with the roles they will play to help me achieve mine.

Preparation becomes a fast-moving activity and very exciting. If you were to watch the whole activity, you would see a lot of interaction between several people at once. We communicate so much with just thought that it requires very little time to piece it all together. Done on Earth, the process would last for several hours with much arguing. We would forget the main goal, the plan, and the lessons. Discussion would become competitive, egos would get in the way, and someone would end up winning or losing in the end. That happens on Earth. In human form, we forget Who We Are and let our egos take over. If we could remember, we wouldn't allow our egos to be so strong, making our way easier. But then would we ultimately learn our lessons?

Here there isn't any of that. Instead, we approach the ritual with much cooperation and love. We *all* win, in a sense. There isn't any judgment over who is better or who has the advantage in a certain situation. We just work together to ensure the presence of possibilities so that each of us can have the best chance of successfully completing our lessons.

I realize this might all sound kind of complicated, but it is simple, really. I will let Areanna tell you more about the process of plotting out the possibilities. Then it's time to meet my soul family and get this started!

Areanna

The Possibilities Board is unlike anything you could create on Earth. As mentioned earlier, it is roughly similar to a board game. However, there are many aspects of the Board that makes it unique and extremely useful for souls that are plotting out their lives.

The Board could best be described like a large sheet of Plexiglas, transparent and flexible. It is approximately two inches thick, and the outer dimensions can range from two feet to thirty feet around, depending on the number of souls working with it. The Board contracts and expands as souls move about the Board. It is not even a flat surface. It can be pushed down or pulled up into various shapes, as needed. Every part of Earth is represented holographically, every road, mountain, river, and town.

Each soul has a token that represents itself. The piece actually resembles the physical body the soul will occupy on Earth, even to the point of taking on the appearance of aging. The token is moved with a thought. Each soul's movement is traced over space and time as defined on Earth. New paths may open and others may close as each soul expresses its desires or choices for its life, including how it might interact with other souls. As the glowing piece moves about the Board, it can become brighter or dimmer as the possibility for a planned lesson becomes more or less of a reality in a certain time or place in the soul's life. A pink light surrounds the token whenever the soul interacts with its soul family members.

Because Sarah is the central character in this particular meeting, her token piece is larger than the rest and more animated. As she moves herself around the Possibilities Board, her token can directly communicate with each soul it comes close to. The two souls discuss the main purpose of their meeting on Earth at this particular time and place.

The level of cooperation is like no other. There is no ego to influence decisions. Each move is made with love, and everyone is mindful of the ultimate goal—Sarah's primary lesson—as well as of secondary lessons that she and other family members will pursue.

As mentioned before, even though the Possibilities Board resembles a game board, there is no competition, no desire for dominance or winning, and no score to keep. There is no right or wrong way, either.

Let's listen in on some of the conversation:

"If I move my piece here, you could move here and set off the chain of events that puts me here. Oh, look! The Board is glowing a little brighter."

"If you could wait until after the encounter with the hurricane, I think this event would have more meaning to me and would test my resolve more."

"Would that be too much to take? It seems like a lot to me. What are your thoughts?"

"If you'll look deep into my eyes at this point, I believe that you'll see Who I Am. That may make a difference in your next move."

"I love you and that is all that matters. I realize that it may be difficult for you to do that, for your soul to knowingly do something that could cause pain for me, but it will be necessary."

"I honor Who You Are and am grateful for your part in this."

As the action is occurring, we Guardian angels are standing in a circle behind our charges, watching and making suggestions when asked. Mostly, though, we allow the soul family to do the planning. We take careful notes on the decisions they make. We (the Guardian and other angels) will meet together to decide how and when we can be of assistance.

In human form, the soul is not always aware of how its life is influenced by the angelic realm, but we have a very important job in assisting the souls to complete their lessons, and we are always there. Having the ability to remember everything that was planned, we are in a unique position in the grand scheme of things. Even the souls, in spirit, are not totally aware of the scope of our influence.

Now let me share with you some of the comments the Guardian angels make to Sarah and her soul family.

"This isn't a race. You don't have to rush through each step."

"Timing can be crucial sometimes."

"If you feel this would be too much pressure on you at that juncture, you still have a choice not to do it. You don't have to do anything if you choose not to."

"This isn't pass/fail. You are not given a grade in the end, remember? You will only be evaluating yourselves on how you did."

"You might judge each other there, but we aren't judging you here. We only observe and serve and love you unconditionally, of course."

"It is totally up to you. Your choices are yours and yours alone."

Playing the Game of Life

If I move here will you be there?
You could jump from place to place
A country road or public square
While we're in the human race

Down this street or up a stair
You could take this parking space
Take a boat or soar through the air
While we're in the human race

Life's just a game you play
With no losers or winners
In the end there won't be
Any saints and sinners

Just play, play nice
Play, play nice

You get to choose where you go
If you need some breathing space
Fight the stream or go with the flow
While we're in the human race

I'm glad you'll be there with me
At some time we will touch base
Glad there's no entrance fee
While we're in the human race

Chapter 10
Final Instructions

*(The spirit) sang its spiritual song for the
child to memorize and use when calling
upon the spirit guardian as an adult.*

—Mourning Dove (Christine Quintasket)

"Areanna," Sarah practically whispers, "I'm getting a little nervous. I'm starting to remember some of the more painful and difficult times I've had on Earth. I know that this is the right thing for me, and I truly want to go, but ... " They quietly sit listening to the birds and waterfalls as Sarah picks absently at her nails.

"What are your concerns, Sarah?" Areanna speaks with kindness and patience.

"I don't really know, I guess. Just the unknown. I know that everything is planned, everything will work for the best, but I'll forget everything again. It's almost like starting from nothing." A butterfly lights on Sarah's hand, and she gently shoos it away.

"You won't be starting completely over, not remembering

anything," Areanna says with a reassuring tone. "Your soul has been through many incarnations, and you have grown and progressed. You are evolving, and that gives you a great beginning."

"I guess I just need another pep talk. Can you tell me again what to expect?" Sarah lifts her eyes to meet Areanna's as furrows crease her brow.

"Of course I will." Taking Sarah's hands in her own, Areanna looks deeply into her eyes as she explains. "When you arrive as a baby, you will still be able to see me and others from the spirit world. Even if your physical body and its senses are not fully functioning and able to be controlled consciously, you will sense us. We will be with you constantly and will communicate with you.

"When you start to babble as a baby, your speech will be verbalized in a way that only we will understand. No one around you in human form will be able to interpret your sounds. There will be many who will play and interact with and mimic you, but it won't make sense to you. It will take years before you can communicate with spoken language.

"We will assist and guide those around you. You know that Beth, as your mother, will be caring for you in a kind, loving way. So will your Earthly father, Joe. They have agreed to give you strong family ties. Joe will be instrumental in helping you with reminders of the Lullaby and the spirit world," Areanna ends and caresses Sarah's cheek.

"Yes, I know that they will love me, and I will love them as well. I am very glad that they agreed to be my parents. I trust them so much," Sarah replies, taking a deep sigh.

"If Beth and Joe are able to remember, they will allow you to have your 'imaginary friends' around you, allow you to speak and interact with us. We can be a great source of comfort in your early years," Areanna says brightly. "There will also be a great deal of interacting with you in your dreams."

"Oh, yes! I remember vivid dreams from other lives that were very helpful," Sarah exclaims. The corners of her mouth curl slightly, and she closes her eyes as she recalls one particular dream. In the dream, she was flying over her problems and laughing while they turned into flowers, with their dried up petals blowing in the wind.

"There are many other ways that I and others will communicate with you. You may not always hear or feel or understand what we are trying to convey, but we are persistent, especially if the message is important. Most of all, Sarah, you will be surrounded with love and peace. When you can feel that, you will know that we are near and hear your every word." Areanna gently puts her arms around Sarah, embracing her with loving arms and wings. A soft pink glow surrounds them. Sarah hears the melody of Lullaby as she breathes deeply the sweet fragrance of Areanna's flowing hair.

"It is so wonderful to have you with me, to feel your presence. I know how much you love me and want what is best for me. Thank you immensely, Areanna. I love you so much," Sarah speaks with a sense of melancholy. Tears well up in her eyes and trace down her cheeks.

Wiping Sarah's tears away, Areanna replies, "I love you, too, Sarah. I always have, and I always will." Then, with strength and conviction, she adds, "Let's complete the last of the preparations before you make your appearance on Earth."

"Yes, let's." Sarah grins widely as the two of them walk arm in arm up the path.

How Will I Know You Are Near?

Areanna

Tell me what you want. What will mean the most to you and I'll do it, but remember, you've got to pay attention.

Sarah (singing)

The soft scent of flowers
The tinkling sound of chimes
A song on the radio where
Messages come in rhymes

Will bring me chills
And when you whisper to me
Inspiration will come to guide me

A touch on my shoulder
Feelings like a hug
Your arms wrapped around me
Knowing the feeling of love

Will bring peace to my heart
And when I feel you near
Your love will come to guide me

Stay close
It may not be so easy this time
Do these things and I'm sure I'll be fine

A kiss on my cheek
As I drift off to sleep
A butterfly going by
Could you come to me in a dream?

That will bring me hope
Then I'll know you're near
And everything you do will guide me

You are my guide, my protector, my friend
Through this life and we will never end
And I will know you're near each time I hear
The Lullaby

CHAPTER 11
THE SEND-OFF

Areanna

This scene has been played out repeatedly, for centuries and longer. Loved ones gather to bid a fond farewell to a small one, going off on a grand adventure. As everyone is focused on one little spirit, anticipation is felt for another time on Earth. Special escorts are in attendance. Angels, guides, and others stand nearby to assist. The soul family is here, of course, except for those who have gone ahead to make preparations for the soul's arrival.

In Sarah's case, Beth and Joe have been incarnated for a couple of decades now. But though their souls are on Earth, their presence is still here. We have been watching their progress toward becoming a loving couple and preparing the new body for Sarah. Soon Sarah will take her place within it and be born in the usual human way, according to the agreed upon plan.

Sarah has made several brief trips to see how her newest physical body has been forming. As planned, it will be a body that will allow her to physically accomplish what her soul has chosen for this incarnation. For what Sarah wants to accomplish, it must be healthy and strong, not too large or small, and definitely feminine. It must be free of anything that would keep her from moving and functioning as she desires.

For this trip, there are no bags to pack. Sarah can take with her only what her soul can carry: love, hope, inspiration, and assorted gifts that she has requested. She may take some memories of the spirit world with her, as well. These memories will include the agreements she has made with her soul family regarding what influence they will have in her life. It is uncertain at this time whether she will eventually forget these memories.

"Sarah, it is almost time," Areanna remarks. "Beth has been in labor, and the time is near for you to arrive."

Sarah is flitting between souls like a little butterfly, making contact with each one. Even David is here, as he would not miss seeing Sarah off on her next adventure. The sense of love and understanding is great, and there is a vast amount of joy and peace. The Lullaby floats all around them, adding beauty to the atmosphere. There is a knowing from all that this plan is perfect.

"Okay, I am ready now." Sarah bravely stands next to Areanna, their lights and essences intermingling and shining brightly. "Just say when and I'm there."

Areanna speaks to the gatherers. "Sarah and I will be leaving now. Our love is with you all."

And with that, the two are surrounded with a brilliant golden light, spherical and pulsing with energy.

* * *

In a small town in western United States, special attending angels, as well as a few soul family members, accompany Sarah to the delivery room.

A fairly new physician, with a look of concern, is encouraging Beth with his words. "Push, Beth. She's almost here. Don't stop pushing. Give it all you can."

Joe, his knees weak and shaky, speaks as bravely as he can. "Come on, Beth. You can do this, I know you can." He is pale, and his forehead is damp with sweat.

Beth is having difficulty focusing. Her blood pressure is dangerously low, and the doctor and nurses are doing what they can to hurry the delivery. Beth, through a fog in her vision, can see the outline of more than just Joe, the doctor, and the nurses all standing before her in that small delivery room.

If she is not mistaken in her weakened state, Beth hears music and ethereal sounds beginning to fill the room. If Beth could describe what she believes she is only imagining, she would say that she sees her grandmother in the corner and others that she does not recognize. Then she sees what appears to be a beautiful young woman with long brown hair, blue eyes, and Joe's smile walking past her on the left. The young woman quickly embraces those around her, and then disappears.

"This is it, Beth. The baby's head is coming. Push!" the doctor yells.

Beth shakes her head to clear it and then gives a final push with every bit of strength she can find. Then she feels relief as a baby's cry fills the air.

Don't Forget the Plan

I'm leaving soon; I'm ready to go
Happy to leave, get on with the show
Gonna do great things, my soul will grow
With you in my life, I'll make it below

You're a part of me so please
Don't forget the plan
Such a part of me
And I can't believe
We're doing this again

(To David)
I'm gonna miss you, wish you'd be there
Making you go would be so unfair
I understand, it's something you won't do
Don't think it strange, but I'll look for you

It's another time
Another life to live
We'll be together
No matter what
It's time to be
Another personality
You'll still be you
And I'll still be me

I know your soul and I know your heart
No matter what, we won't be apart
Angels will guide us through dark and light
No matter what, it's gonna turn out right

EPILOGUE

"Good morning, Sarah. Aren't you looking pretty today in your new outfit? It's your very first Christmas, and it will be so fun."

Joe takes Sarah from her crib. He has forgotten how many times he has been a mother and a father in other lives, and how well he cares for children, so he handles her delicately. He is learning again, and his Guardian angel, Kamali, watches over him with amusement.

Sarah, trying to focus on Joe's face, curves up her bottom lip just slightly, and Joe lets out a whoop. "Beth, come and look! Sarah is smiling!"

Beth runs into the nursery. "What? Is everything okay? What is wrong?"

"Nothing. I'm sorry if I frightened you. Sarah just smiled!"

"Well, of course she did." Beth looks down at Sarah. "You sweet thing, you." Beth and Joe smile and laugh. Sarah lets out a little startled cry at the commotion.

"Oh, Joe. I forgot to tell you that a package came yesterday from your Great Aunt Misty."

"Any idea what it might be?"

"No, but it is heavy and sounds like rocks when I shake it."

"That's probably exactly what it is. You know how Misty loves crystals. Come on, Sarah. Let's go find out. It's time to start opening the presents."

Areanna and Mesha follow along, moving unseen by everyone but Sarah.

"I'm glad that the crystals arrived. Now Sarah can start benefiting from them," Areanna says.

"Yes," replied Mesha, "and Joe and Beth, too."

ABOUT THE AUTHOR

Patti Angeletti lives in Boise, Idaho. She is the author of *Rising Above Organized Religion* (iUniverse), and her lyrics have been used in recordings by Dunes Boys. When not working as a registered nurse or traveling, she enjoys her children and grandchildren. She continues to seek a deeper meaning to life.

GLOSSARY

There are many topics of a metaphysical or new age nature mentioned in this book. I have listed them below. I encourage you to discover your own belief system and truths regarding these and other topics by searching outside of yourself in books, libraries, and the Internet. Ask questions of others, attend classes, and participate in lively discussions. Most of all, I encourage you to seek truth within your own heart and soul and use discernment.

Angels: Spiritual beings believed to act as attendants, agents, or messengers.

Archangels: Angels of high rank.

Astrology: The study of the movements and relative positions of celestial bodies and the interpretation of their influence on human affairs and the natural world.

Chakras: Centers of spiritual power in the human body.

Connectedness: Joining together with others in a sense of relatedness.

Contracts and agreements: Negotiated arrangements between parties as to certain courses of action.

Creating: Bringing something into existence.

Duality: The quality or condition of being dual.

Free will: The Power to act without the constraint of necessity or fate; the ability to act at one's own discretion

God: Creator of the Universe, the Supreme Being. *See also* Higher Power.

Hierarchy of angels: A system in which angels are ranked one above the other according to status or authority. This is the traditional system of order among angels and other heavenly beings.

Higher Power: Creator of the Universe, the Supreme Being. *See also* God.

Manifesting: Causing something to happen as a result of one's actions.

Numerology: The branch of knowledge that deals with the occult significance of numbers.

Reincarnation: The rebirth of a soul in a new body.

Soul: The spiritual part of a human being, regarded as immortal.

Spirit: A person's moral or emotional nature or sense of identity.

Resources

Doreen Virtue
    www.angeltherapy.com
    Books: *Angels 101: An Introduction to Connecting, Working,*
        and Healing with the Angels
    Archangels & Ascended Masters
    Messages from Your Angels

Robert Schwartz
    www.yoursoulsplan.com
    Books: *Courageous Souls*
    Your Soul's Plan

Betty J. Eadie
    www.embracedbythelight.com
    Books: *Embraced by the Light*
    The Awakening Heart

Sylvia Browne
    www.sylvia.org

Books: *Spiritual Connections: How to Find Spirituality throughout All the Relationships in Your Life*
Exploring the Levels of Creation
Contacting Your Spirit Guide

Brian Weiss, MD
www.brianweiss.com
Books: *Many Souls, Many Masters*
Through Time into Healing
Only Love Is Real
Messages from the Masters
Same Soul, Many Bodies

Michael Newton, PhD
www.spiritualregression.org
Books: *Journey of Souls*
Destiny of Souls

Printed in the United States
by Baker & Taylor Publisher Services